A Perfect Match

Written by Kitty Richards
Illustrated by Olga Mosqueda and Charles Pickens

A Random House PICTUREBACK® Book

Random House 🏠 New York

ISBN: 978-0-7364-2892-7
randomhouse.com/kids
Printed in the United States of America

10 9 8 7 6 5 4 3 2 1

Pixie Hollow is unlike any other place. The seasons exist side by side all year long! But the warm-weather fairies were told not to go into the Winter Woods, where the winter fairies live. It was simply too cold for their warm fairy wings. Most of the warm-weather fairies listened. All except *one*.

It was a busy day in Pixie Hollow. All the tinker fairies were making snowflake baskets to be delivered to the winter fairies.

"That should be enough to finish the baskets," Tinker Bell said, dropping off a batch of leaves. Once all the baskets were done, snowy owls would fly them to the Winter Woods.

Tink wished she could go to the Winter Woods, too. "I can't believe we make the baskets but we don't get to take them to the winter fairies," she complained to her friends Bobble and Clank.

"We wouldn't last a day in that cold," Bobble said.

A few minutes later, Tinker Bell spotted her friend Fawn, an animal fairy. Fawn was taking animals across the border to the Winter Woods. Tink volunteered to help.

At the border, Tinker Bell looked across to the beautiful, snow-covered world. While Fawn was trying to wake a sleeping marmot, Tink jumped across!

Suddenly, Tink's wings began to glow and sparkle. *"Whoa,"* she said in awe.

It was amazing, thrilling, unexpected...and very, very strange!

Fawn quickly yanked Tinker Bell back across the border. "Your wings—they're *freezing*!" Fawn cried.

But Tinker Bell was too curious about what had just happened to worry about being cold. What had made her wings sparkle?

After a healing-talent fairy helped warm her wings, Tink headed to the library to do some research. She found what she was looking for—a book about wings. But a bookworm had eaten through some of the pages she needed!

Tink was told that she could learn more from the Keeper, who lived in the Winter Woods. There was only one thing for Tink to do. . . .

First, Tinker Bell cut a warm
winter coat out of a fuzzy leaf.

Next, she made a pair
of furry snow boots.

Then she packed the rest of
her things in a satchel.

Fully dressed for the cold,
Tink tried to fly. But
with her wings tucked
inside her coat, she
fell right over. Good
thing she had a
backup plan!

Tink would get to the Winter Woods by hiding in one of the snowflake baskets! She snuck into a basket and hid. Then a snowy owl grabbed the basket and flew off! It was a very bumpy ride.

Soon, Tink arrived in the Winter Woods. There was just one problem—her book had fallen out of her satchel! A winter fairy spotted the book and picked it up. Tink secretly followed him.

The winter fairy headed to the Hall of Winter. Tinker Bell gasped as she went inside. The grand icy chamber was packed with books chiseled out of ice!

Just then, Tink spotted the Keeper. He was hard at work, carving books at his easel.

"Keeper! Keeper!" Tink suddenly heard a winter fairy say. "The most amazing thing happened! You've got to tell me what it means!"

"My wings, they actually lit up!" the winter fairy exclaimed. Her name was Periwinkle. "And it's happening again!"

Just then, Tink's wings began to sparkle, too! She tossed her coat aside and stepped forward in surprise. The two fairies approached each other as their wings shimmered.

The Keeper, whose name was Dewey, shook his head in disbelief. He had never seen anything like this before. "I've only heard of this...," he began. "Follow me!"

Dewey guided the girls onto a giant snowflake. When a ribbon of light passed through Tink and Peri's wings, an image of a baby laughing projected onto the icy wall. Then the laugh split in two. One half headed to the warm part of Pixie Hollow, and the other half headed toward winter.

Tinker Bell's eyes widened. "Two fairies born of the same laugh. So that means we're. . ."

She and Peri looked at each other in awe. *"SISTERS!"* they exclaimed in unison.

The sisters couldn't wait to learn all about each other.
They had a lot of catching up to do!

"I'm a frost fairy. I frost things," Peri said.
"And I'm Tinker Bell. I'm a tinker. I . . ."
"*Tinker* things?" Peri asked, giggling.

Peri and Tink discovered they had a lot in common! They both liked to wear white pom-poms on their shoes.

They both liked to collect Lost Things—although Periwinkle called them *Found* Things.

They also both liked butterflies. Or at least Peri was sure she would, if she ever got to see one!

And Tink and Peri's favorite star? The Second Star to the Right, of course!

Later, Periwinkle took Tinker Bell on a tour of the Winter Woods. Tink was amazed by the wintry world her sister lived in.

They went ice-skating . . .

. . . and ice-sliding!

Then they visited the Frost Forest. They watched frost fairies spinning frost as delicate as the finest lace, and snowflake fairies creating beautiful, icy snowflakes.

A little while later, the moon began to rise and the air grew colder. It was time for Tinker Bell to return home.

"Good-bye, Peri," Tink said, giving her sister a hug.

But they were not sad. They both knew it wasn't really good-bye. They were sisters, born of the same laugh. And nothing could keep them apart.